With thanks and praises for the Great Mystery *R.R.*

May every child in this world find real happiness
and peace in his or her life *D.K.*

Text copyright © 2006 Rachel Rivett
Illustrations copyright © 2006 Dubravka Kolanovic
This edition copyright © 2006 Lion Hudson

The moral rights of the author and illustrator
have been asserted

A Lion Children's Book
an imprint of
Lion Hudson plc
Mayfield House, 256 Banbury Road,
Oxford OX2 7DH, England
www.lionhudson.com
ISBN-13 978 0 7459 4909 3
ISBN-10 0 7459 4909 6

First edition 2006
1 3 5 7 9 10 8 6 4 2 0

A catalogue record for this book is available
from the British Library

Typeset in Caslon Oldface BT 18/24
Printed and bound in China

Little Grey
and the Great Mystery

Rachel Rivett

Dubravka Kolanovic

LION
CHILDREN'S

Little Grey uncurled himself from his tail and slipped
out of his dreaming with a question to ask.
   'Grandmother,' he said eagerly, 'what do you know
of the Great Mystery from where we all come?'
   'Ahhh,' said Old Grey, 'that is a very large
wondering, little one. You are a gatherer,
Little Grey. Go and see if you can gather
some answers to your wondering.'

Little Grey ran out along the branch. He stopped to watch the spiralling dance of the crows.

'Sister Crow,' he called, 'can you tell me, please, what you know of the Great Mystery?'

The crow alighted next to him. 'For us, the Great Mystery is like the wind that we love so much. When we stretch our wings and fly, we trust him to catch us. On our own we fly, but with the wind…' She threw back her head and *CAAWED*.

Little Grey sat and watched the crows riding the invisible currents for a long time.

At last he called his thanks and rippled down the tree. As the sun rose across the sky, he played beside the stream.

'Brother Stream,' he said, 'can you tell me, please, what you know of the Great Mystery?'

The stream flowed strongly through the rocks.

'For us, the Great Mystery is like the sea that we love so much. Every stream, every raindrop, every cloud remembers there is a place where we are one. And we journey to her. Our adventures are many and wondrous. But only when we reach the sea can all the water of the world be one.'

Little Grey thanked the stream and sat for a long time listening to the song of his journey.

At last he joined his friends tumbling through the beech nuts beneath the trees.

When the light faded, Little Grey waved goodbye to his friends and returned to his home tree.

He looked up at the mighty beech and asked, 'Father Tree, can you tell me, please, what you know of the Great Mystery?'

The beech tree rustled his sunset leaves. 'For us, the Great Mystery is like the seasons that we love so much, for they show us our true nature: in winter, we let our precious leaves go and seem to let go of all we are; then we find we are clothed with the sky itself, and instead of leaves we wear the stars.'

Little Grey watched a pale yellow leaf flutter slowly down, and in its place a star appeared in the vastness of the growing dark. He chewed his tail thoughtfully and then thanked the tree, and ran swiftly down the trunk to his hole.

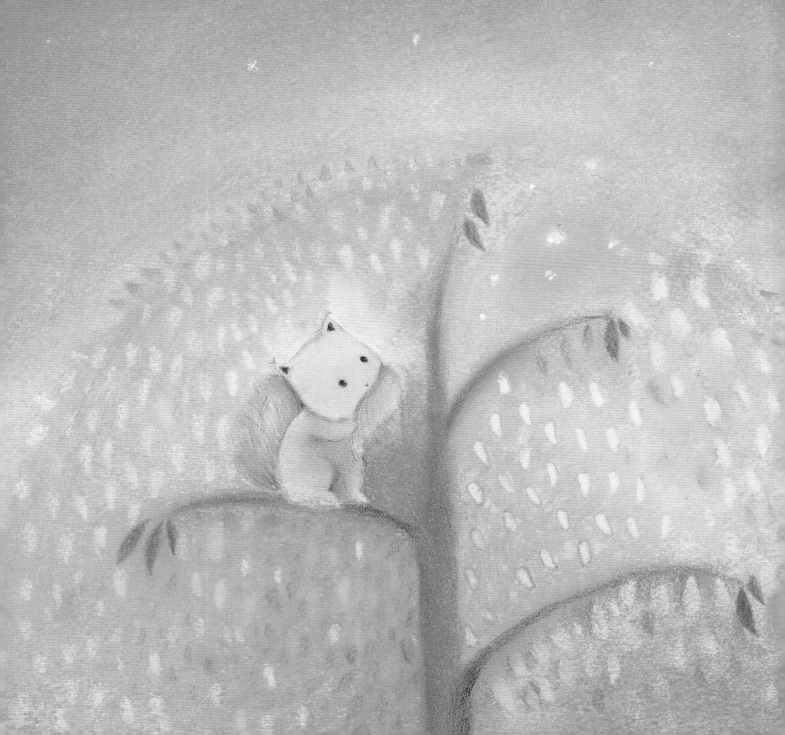

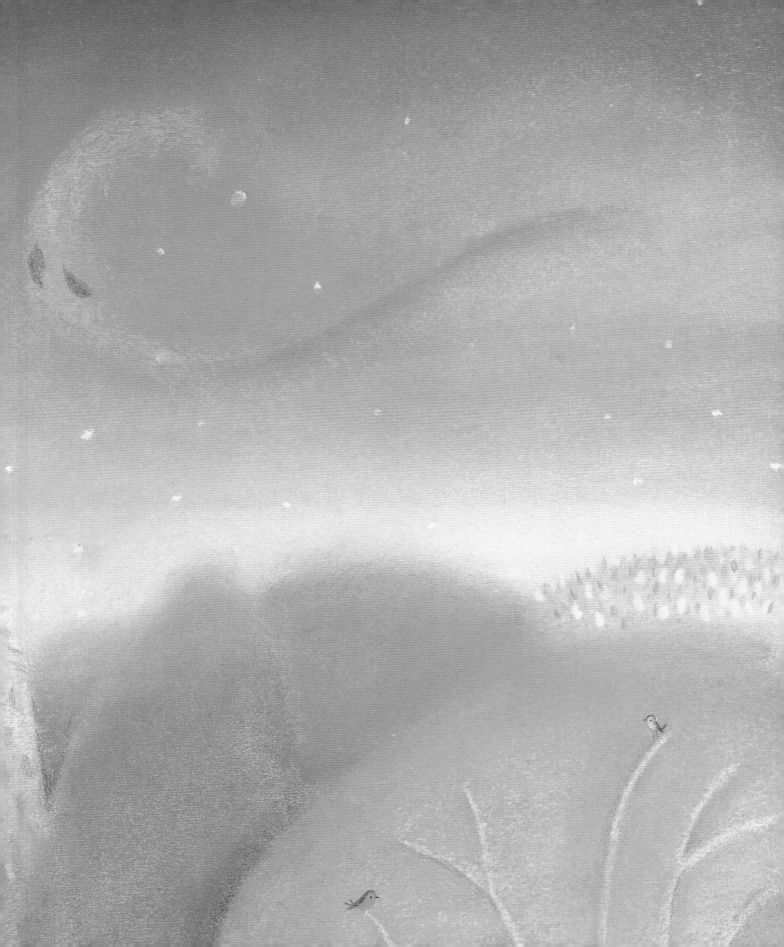

Before he went inside, he stopped and watched the full moon climbing into the sky.

'Grandmother Moon, can you tell me, please, what you know of the Great Mystery?'

The moon touched him gently with her silver light. 'For me, the Great Mystery is like the sun who I love so much, for he fills us all with the light of his love. Did you know, little one, that I return the sun's light to him as a gift? And when we move through the heavens in our circular dance, I live and die and am born again; all in the light of our love.'

Little Grey sat in the glow of evening as the clouds darkened from pink to mauve to grey and asked himself: 'Well, Little Grey, can *you* tell me, please, what *you* know of the Great Mystery?' Thoughtfully he scratched his chin with his paw. 'What do I love best?' he asked himself, and then he smiled.

'For me, the Great Mystery must be like the tree who I love so much, and in which I live. He shelters me from storms and feeds me with his nuts, and I return to him to rest. I would be an earth creature were it not for the tree, but his roots and trunk and branches let me climb from earth, to sky, and back to earth again, as often as I wish.'

He hugged the broad body of the tree fiercely and turned a little somersault before scampering into his hole.

Old Grey was waiting for him.

'Well, little one, have you had good gatherings?'

Little Grey hugged her. 'For Sister Crow, the Great Mystery is like the wind; for Brother Stream, the Great Mystery is like the sea; for Father Tree, the Great Mystery is like the seasons; and for Grandmother Moon, the Great Mystery is like the sun. And for me, the Great Mystery is like the tree.'

Old Grey nodded. 'So, Little Grey. Are there then many of the Great Mystery, or is it that for each of us the Great Mystery is different?'

Little Grey snuggled into his tail. 'I am not sure, but I think it may be that each of us comes to know the Great Mystery through what we love best; and it is different because each of us is different.'

Old Grey nodded and snuggled down beside him. 'I wonder then, if all of us together might learn to know a little more of the Great Mystery than we can on our own.'

Little Grey yawned and closed his eyes. 'Yes, I wonder,' he said, and slipped away into his dreaming.

Then Old Grey leaned across him and whispered, 'Thank you Little Grey, that was a good day's gathering.' And as the moon rose and shone her gift of light into the darkness, she softly kissed him goodnight.